The Cranny

By Vincent James Vezza

Copyright © 2018 by Vincent James Vezza

ISBN 13: 978-1986395595
ISBN 10: 1986395596

All rights reserved. No part of this publication may be reproduced in any form, or by any means, electronic or mechanical, including photocopying, recording, or any information browsing, storage, or retrieval systems, without permission in writing from the author.

Published by Hidden Treasure Novels

Cover art created by Amber Fritz
Initial cover concept developed by Sharon Upton
Front and back cover final design produced by Michelle L. Baptiste-Perez
Editing by Chelly Peeler of Ink It Out Editing Services

Chapter 1
A New Discovery

On the western bank of the Dutch Buffalo Creek, I gazed at a slow-swirling cranny. It was isolated from the rivulet that continued to flow a normal course on its way to the sea. There were so many similar ponds formed by the receding water, starved by a lack of replenishing rain.

Just below the surface, ten tadpoles circled a blade buried in the mud of a distant past. Above them, a turtle was drawn to the warmth of the high noon sun. A frog struggled to mount a leaf that drifted on the waterline. I wondered if this submerged creation knew about life beyond the cranny. Would they find a way back to the creek that left them forsaken in this isolated pool?

Then their voices entered my mind's ear. The first of the ten spoke. "Brothers and sisters, look at our cousin floating toward that light."

The second responded, "Yes, maybe he thinks it will provide warmth."

The third said, "I think he believes it will provide food."

The fourth chimed in, "Turtles are like that; they'll come out of their shell for a little ray of hope, a degree of heat, or the lure of nourishment."

"We know better," said the fifth tadpole. "It is quite acceptable to circle the bottom water. We have no need to pursue those elements in our present form."

The sixth chastised them, "Don't be judgmental. Our cousin is drifting toward a world that we will enter someday soon."

"Not in our present form," said the seventh. "Not in these aquatic bodies. We'll need to shed these tails and assume different bodies to survive above the waterline."

Then I heard the eighth reveal his thoughts, "Cousin Turtle and Uncle Frog perceive the universe from a different point of view. Turtle told me that he could see the light more clearly when he surfaced. He said that there is a world out there framed by blue skies and puffy white clouds. Shrubs and trees and flowers paint the landscape. There's plenty to eat and life-giving oxygen comes from the air."

Number nine said, "Too scary, I don't want to give up my body. I'm fine with getting my nourishment from the muddy bottom water. The light doesn't interest me a bit."

Number ten responded, "You'll change your mind when you learn how to hop, skip, and jump. You'll learn to love the light. By the way, this cranny will be swept away by the next heavy rain. The creek will consume this temporary home. You'll need a new life to weather the impending storm."

Then, Uncle Frog spoke. "Follow the light—stop drifting in endless circles. The Progenitor will give a new meaning to your existence. Look at the blade you circle. There are many others like it left behind in the muddy water of life."

I pulled the rusty blade from their home. The turtle and the frog moved to opposite shores. The tadpoles continued to circle the newly created crevice that slowly disappeared under the weight of sinking sand.

That moment reminded me of a similar gathering that took place just upstream. Maybe there was a treasure to be found in the lives of these little ones. In a different cranny, ten other tadpoles created a metaphorical parallel universe in **The Hidden Treasure of Dutch Buffalo Creek**, an award-winning novel I read over a year ago. This year, yet another army of related tadpoles surfaced in a sequel novella titled **Neverborn**.

In the novel, the other tadpoles circled a different bayonet, placed in this same creek by a Hessian soldier many tadpole years ago. In the novella, the new tadpoles paid tribute to the voices of never-born souls.

When I returned to the house, I cleaned the bayonet. Years of mud drained into a bright orange five-gallon bucket. I retrieved the novel and novella from my book collection in the den and began to read the stories again.

The novel opened my eyes to a whole new universe. It helped me to see the world through the eyes of never-born children. It allowed me to hear their voices. They observed and recorded events that were left stranded on the shores of recorded history. The novella brought focus to the possibility of another realm.

Following my read, I returned to the creek. The tadpoles

still circled about in the water. Perhaps they were unaware that the blade was no longer there. I closed my eyes and tried to hear their voices. This time, I could imagine calling them by name.

Their names would underpin those given to their predecessors: Anna, Bernadette, Christopher, Daniel, Elizabeth, Frederick, George, Henry, Israel, and Jackson.

Anna was the first voice that I heard. She whispered, "So good to know that now we actually have names. Someone out there recognizes that we are creatures worthy of note."

Bernadette reinforced her sister's observation. "Yes, we circle about in a world that most people never see. Maybe that's just as well, less chance to be spotted by predators who think of us as dinner."

Christopher added to the dialogue. "Makes sense, but why do I have a masculine name?"

Daniel responded, "Our names aren't provided for our benefit. They are assigned to represent the souls who will pick up our mantle long after we have been transformed."

Elizabeth flipped her tail and delivered her thoughts. "We're all caught up in the same circle of life. Only the Progenitor really knows how we fit into the scheme of creation."

Frederick, caught in her wake, ventured to share, "I could draw analogies between tadpoles and humans who never have a chance to draw breath into their lungs."

George seconded the statement. "Maybe I could give each potential human a name."

At that moment, I opened my eyes and thought about a paragraph in the novel. The author, Jackson Badgenoone, *pronounced Badge-No-One*, quoted Isaiah 43:1–3. Then she ended the story with another verse from the same book, Isaiah 45:3.

> *"I will give you hidden treasures,*
> *riches stored in secret places,*
> *so that you may know that I am the* LORD,
> *the God of Israel, who summons you by name."*

*[Jackson amplified her message in **Neverborn**.]*

Henry interrupted my thoughts. "I suppose everyone deserves a name. How else would the world know about our individual contribution?"

Israel was quick to respond. "You don't get it; our name is of secondary consequence."

After hearing the dialogue between those aquatic brothers, I reflected again on my reading from both of Jackson's works. In the novella she reveals that people are called by the name of their creator. Jackson quoted 2 Chronicles 7:14.

> *"If my people, who are called **by my name**, will humble themselves and pray and seek my face and turn from their wicked ways, then I will hear from heaven, and I will forgive their sin and will heal their land."*

At that moment this new Jackson, the Jackson of *this* cranny, delivered her assessment. "Israel got it right. In time, no one will remember our names. Our bodies will morph into another form. Our souls will follow along."

That evening, I returned to the den and resumed reading the book titled **Neverborn**. The principal character, a woman named Rachael, is the personification of a modern-day female Job.

Rachael finds support from several women who suffer through similar trials; the loss of children born sleeping and the untimely death of loved ones. The voice of her never-born child encourages Rachael to share a message that carries her through all the difficult circumstances. She ultimately challenges readers to consider what gives them comfort in times of turmoil and grief.

The challenges faced by Rachael and her circle of family and friends resonate with countless women down through the ages. Husbands and dads feel the pain from a different perspective. Jackson Badgenoone considered both vantage points when she wrote through the sorrow and recovery revealed in the story.

Chapter 2
A New Voice

The following day I obtained a newly-released audio book version of **The Hidden Treasure of Dutch Buffalo Creek**. The narrator brought a new dimension to the novel. His voice captured a cadence that brought the words to life. I listened to the first few paragraphs.

"The creek bed was nearly dry, a rivulet with barely a stir. Thirty feet beneath the western ridge, ten feet east of where the cool water kissed the muddy western bank, a glint of silver reflected skyward from a shallow, slow-swirling cranny."

The story continued to unfold. "Beneath the surface, ten tadpoles circled about their temporary aquatic home. With a gentle tug, the submerged portion of the object began to appear, releasing a cloud of silt. The amphibians scattered to each of the four points on a compass."

Adam Hanin, the narrator, delicately revealed how an aging man named James discovered a bayonet buried in the seasonally shallow creek. The blade led James to sift through a lifetime of artifacts and bittersweet memories. He found riches from the past and caught a glimpse of the future. Just as the bayonet glimmered in the depth of the water, so did the ongoing work of his family's unseen witnesses, the never-born. They revealed treasures that went far beyond mere gold and silver.

The audio book benefitted from the same experimental literature structure. Both were constructed in a book within a book format. Select sanitized chapters permitted the author to present very adult themes to a receptive young audience. That new audience could peek back in time, into the world of Baby Boomers, the Greatest Generation, the flappers and their predecessors.

Each generation came to grips with the station of existence. Unlike the tadpoles, humans could weave a written historical thread that bonded the years, decades, and centuries of life. Tadpoles only knew what they heard. They only heard what I allowed them to hear.

As I continued to listen to Jackson's novel, I discovered the undercurrents of civilization. **The Hidden Treasure of Dutch Buffalo Creek** brought to life symbols that successive generations could appreciate. Boomers – the music of The Beatles. The Greatest Generation – the music of Glenn Miller, and so on back in time.

Each gathering of new souls had an opportunity to repudiate the bayonet as an instrument of death, and to accept the golden ring as a symbol of life. The never-born observers in the novel were there to see it all.

Adam's voice melted away the hours. He hoisted the historical anchors in every chapter to reveal spiritual underpinnings. Taking cues from the written words, he changed the cadence and tone to reflect the subtle shift in focus.

A few days later, I returned to the creek. The tadpoles continued to stir the stagnant water. Bernadette seemed to stare at me as she momentarily left the tadpole army circle. For a moment, I could read her mind.

"Why do you stare at me that way? Just because I can't write or read doesn't mean that I can't think."

Without hesitation, I responded to her non-verbal challenge. "So maybe we could just mind-meld our thoughts; you–little tadpole, and me–the old man that I've become."

She raced through my cerebral cortex. "You can believe in the voices of never-born; why are you surprised that I have a story to tell?

"I know about the novella that you're reading and the novel that captures your ear. The novel began as a modest attempt to explain away the passage of time, keeping alive the memories of an entire clan. The novella does a deep dive into tragedy that visits everyone born of human flesh.

"We tadpoles have our fair share of trouble, too; we don't dwell on them the way you do. We know that someday we will have to leave the security of this cranny. We look forward to the day when we become frogs, able to breathe and feel the full warm sun. But the thought of change scares us just as much as it scares you."

Bernadette darted back into the army. Christopher picked

up her dialogue. "Old man, you keep alive memories of people too soon forgotten and events that melt away like snow. Will the Millennials of your species care much about any of them?"

"They will when they realize the impact of those lives and events on their world. ***The Hidden Treasure of Dutch Buffalo Creek*** reveals nuggets of encouragement not found in any other venue. Sequel novella, ***Neverborn***, provides a road map to dealing with unspeakable grief that visits every population."

"What about us, old man? Who will write our stories?"

I watched Christopher as he returned to his place in the circle and said, "I will, Christopher. I'll tell your story. You and your siblings deserve a place at the table. I even have a working title for the story. I'll call it ***The Cranny***."

Frederick suggested that I start with a short story and then consider a more ambitious format. Before I could respond to his suggestion, a drop of rain interrupted my thoughts. Then another drop fell, and another. Within a few minutes, the sky opened up and released a torrent. Within hours, the creek rose and overcame the cranny. The little tadpoles were washed downstream. I didn't have an opportunity to properly say goodbye, but I would keep alive their memory and anticipate meeting them again.

Chapter 3
Expanded Reading

That evening, I returned to my den and retrieved the printed copy of the novel that I read more than a year ago, ***The Hidden Treasure of Dutch Buffalo Creek***. Having heard the word perhaps with a second read, I could learn more about the little tadpoles from the ancestors described in the very first chapter of that novel. I began reading.

Beacon for Tadpoles
"The creek bed was nearly dry, a rivulet with barely a stir. Thirty feet beneath the western ridge, ten feet east of where the cool water kissed the muddy western bank, a glint of silver reflected skyward from a shallow, slow-swirling cranny.

It was a warm summer day in 2014, Anno Domini, A.D., a year of reflection and reconciliation. At high noon, a beacon of sunlight danced through the leaves of a sweet gum tree. A focused ray silhouetted an object in the water below. Up closer, it appeared more like gold; perhaps it *was* gold.

Just a few miles to the southeast, gold was discovered in another rocky creek bed. That find led to the formation of the first commercial gold mine in the United States. The mine produced enough ore to prompt the establishment of a mint in the neighboring city of Charlotte, North Carolina.

It was not long after the founding of the new country, and not long before a conflict that would test the foundation of that republic. To this day, children at heart from near and far continue to sift with metal pans for nuggets of gold at the Reed Gold Mine.

Two books, **Golden Promise in the Piedmont: The Story of John Reed's Mine** and **The Carolina Gold Rush**, describe in some detail how the mine came into being. They also consider the impact it had on the local economy and the emergence of a growing national obsession. The object shimmering in the water demanded attention." Page 1

[I wondered how many crannies were formed by the receding creeks that cut ribbons through the Carolina Piedmont. I continued to read.]

"A rope was anchored to a maple tree, wound three times around the trunk. It stretched another fifty feet, more than sufficient to lower to the edge below, and halfway to the eastern bank. Dust plumes rose as boot-clad feet pressed into the parched brown mud and dull orange clay; the feet then made a cautious descent to the water.

Above the surface, a cylindrical object stood guard; it was about three inches high, with a diameter not much greater than that of a Roman Denarius. It was not gold, nor silver, but it *was* some sort of metal. Beneath the surface, ten tadpoles circled about their temporary aquatic home.

With a gentle tug, the submerged portion of the object began to appear, releasing a cloud of silt. The amphibians scattered to each of four points on a compass. They would assume terrestrial bodies on land based north, southeast, southwest and west of the creek.

It was a bayonet. Lifted gently, the blade glistened inch by inch, with nearly another twenty added to the three above the surface. It slowly rose from the watery grave that held it captive for so long. Intense curiosity overcame disappointment when an old man named James was reminded that *all that glitters is not gold.*

How long it had been there — or how it got there — was anyone's speculation. Most likely it hailed from the War of Northern Aggression or the War of Southern Secession. The color of the uniform labeled the cause. Future historians would refer to it as the Civil War.

The bayonet might have been manufactured in North Carolina. A USA or CSA label could have been engraved in the blade, incidental to the year it was forged.

It might have been crafted in England and left in the mud by a soldier in the service of King George III two generations earlier. Perhaps it had been polished in Germany, Italy or Japan and surrendered to time by a veteran returning to his home a century later. Years and corrosion had wiped clean any evidence of origin." Page 2

[*I wondered if that bayonet bore any resemblance to the blade I retrieved from my cranny, I continued reading.*]

"The moment that the tip of the bayonet touched the

summer air, a forceful gust of wind caught the uppermost boughs of a strand of southern pine. It filtered through seven hundred and fifty thousand green pine-scented needles, then through fifty-five thousand bitternut hickory leaves.

Gaining additional voice as it travelled along the forest floor, it then became a gentle wisp that drifted to the west. She brought moist refreshment to the parched path, revealing her name in the echo of the breeze.

Jackson's apparition whispered. *The national origin of this glittering iron has no more meaning. It was once a source of pride, possibly an instrument of death. Now it is a low water marker, destined for den, country auction, Craigslist or eBay.*

James brushed aside her voice, wiped off the mud, and brought the blade back to his den.

Within days, rains returned, and the creek rose to a new level. It spilled into the recently-harvested corn fields. Dry brown stalks disappeared beneath the rising blue tide. Neighbors bragged that they acquired lakefront property several times each year when Dutch Buffalo Creek satisfied her flood plain. They marked the high water with wooden or plastic stakes and wondered if the next rise would threaten their homes.

The bayonet claimed a different kind of wonderment. Perhaps the bones of two soldiers, one the victor, the other vanquished, rested with each other in a peaceful meadow near a meandering creek, covered with clover, scented with wild flowers. Songbirds would provide a perfect serenade under a Carolina blue sky.

The metal yielded no flesh, no bone. Water and time had also washed away any blood from this blade. Maybe this bayonet wasn't used to kill a soldier.

Bayonets were originally fashioned for hunting, not war. Perhaps it staved off a black bear, a panther or a wolf. Perhaps it served as a convenient metal rod to measure the melt of snow in decades long ago.

It was wishful thinking on his part. The heart of man was bent on conflict. He confirmed that notion by placing the blade alongside an illustrated documentary work. *Battle, A Visual Journey Through 5000 Years of Combat* was literally and figuratively the heaviest book in the den overlooking Dutch Buffalo Creek.

James sat in his favorite chair and ran his hand through pepper gray hair. His mind conjured fanciful possibilities. He imagined that the bayonet was placed in a crevice formed by the displacement of a gold-laden rock.

Maybe it was positioned as a pointer to a hidden treasure. Anger knotted in his throat. He had not taken the time to record the direction of the socket base. He was certain that the tip of the blade pointed downward into the mud, giving him a sinking suspicion that this artifact harbored broader wealth.

Nuggets of truth, any relevance for the dead or living, would require sifting through a screen of events. Sifting for the truth and relevance of the bayonet would prove more arduous than sifting for precious metal. He chose the easier search: a return to the creek as soon as the water receded."
Page 4

[The description of James reminded me of a dear man named Henry, who became an instant friend during my rehabilitation following surgery. Like James, Henry had pepper-gray hair. Henry was forever talking about looking for gold. My thoughts drifted to a

conversation that we had at the rehabilitation center.]

"Vincent, if I ever get to leave this rehab center, I'm going back to the creek to pan for gold. Did you ever pan for gold?"

"I did, Henry, a couple of times, when my grandchildren came to visit."

"So, did you find any nuggets?"

"No, Henry, just a few flakes that settled to the bottom of the pan."

"Well, Vincent, if you piece enough of those flakes together you could have yourself a little set-aside money."

"Henry, at my age and after what I've gone through, I'd be looking for a different kind of treasure. Henry, what would you really like to do?"

"I already have a head start on that, Vincent. I plan to write a book. I thought about sharing an experience I had down by the creek that runs behind my house. My book would be designed for all ages. To invite children to the story, I would share a time when I discovered some tadpoles circling in still water. For the adult readers, I would do a deep dive into the meaning of life."

[Long ago I came to believe that there is no such thing as coincidence in the journey of life. Henry's aspiration was similar to that of Jackson Badgenoone. The difference, of course, is that Henry was never able to complete his story. I tried to imagine how he would have constructed his plot. In the meantime, I returned to Jackson's novel and resumed reading.]

"On his (James) next trek through the woods, Jackson made her presence felt once again. She encouraged him to postpone another descent in search for gold. He marked the high water and the place where he had heard her voice for the second time.

He (James) agreed. There would be time enough to search for any precious metal sheltered in the bottom water. He paused to consider the high water markers. They were anchored shallow and deep, narrow and wide. They were a measure of change for oceans, rivers, streams, creeks and civilizations. He would first seek their meaning.

Throughout time, they served as reminders of the possible, of what was and what might be again. This creek would ebb and crest with the same regularity that visits the rise and fall of people, men and women, industries, nations, and empires."
Page 4

[*As I continued to read, I discovered that James really believed that the voice of Jackson was real. She gently guided him to widen the search for the meaning of the bayonet. The broader search led James to sift through a treasure trove of artifacts, letters and books, which lined the shelves in his den.*]

Ironically for James, some of the books and letters revealed truths about his family, truths that he had never considered. In addition to her role as narrator, Jackson also managed to guide the readings, concealing some truths that were better left hidden for the time.

Jackson asked James to focus on ten books in particular. Nine books considered the lives of his immediate family members. A tenth examined the life of a distant relative. Jackson constructed a scenario where each book was labeled with standard numeration. The chapters within each book were identified by using Roman numerals.

Since only selected sanitized chapters would find a way into the master book, the structural convention made some sense. It would be awkward to have three mentions of a chapter X independent of book number. With the number, the chapter headings could stand apart; Book 4 Chapter X, Book 5 Chapter X, Book 7 Chapter X, and so on.

The construction also enabled Jackson, the author, to draw some interesting lines to the foundations of western civilization, at least back to the days of the Roman Empire. She was, after all, developing translucent memoirs based in the framework of historical fiction.

[I wondered if Henry would have constructed a similar plot line for his book. I breezed through several more chapters. That evening and for several more I continued reading. Later in the week, I returned to the creek. The water had receded and new crannies were formed. I couldn't contain my joy when I saw a new army of tadpoles. I immediately began to communicate with them.]

Chapter 4
A New Generation

"Good morning, little tadpoles, can you hear me?"

There was no response. Did they not speak to me or could I no longer hear their voices? I watched as they darted about in the shallow pool and counted their number. There were twelve in this cranny. I closed my eyes and tried to imagine if they were somehow related to the ten who had been swept away by the flood. Then I heard them, and at once knew that they could hear me.

"Have you any names for us, old man?

I opened my eyes, too late to recognize the tadpole who challenged me at that moment.

"For now I'll refer to you by number."

One called out, "Can I be number one?"

"No, that tadpole number was assigned to one of your kind who lived in another cranny. She was numbered with nine siblings. You can be number 11. Others in your tadpole army of twelve can be identified as 12, 13, 14, 15, 16, 17, 18, 19, 20, 21, and 22."

Number Eleven replied, "That's fine. Maybe someday I'll meet up with Number Seven. Together we could form a lucky pair."

I watched number eleven break away from the circle, and addressed him directly. "There's no such thing as luck. In any event, even if you meet Number Seven, chances are you won't have much in common. He has a name now, and he no longer shares your form. Maybe after you emerge as a new creature you'll be able to understand."

Number Sixteen joined the conversation. "Old man, do you refer to George? I heard that he went on to accomplish a lot of good things in his frog life. He taught his brothers and sisters how to remain still and silent on a lily pad. He was the first of his army to fully appreciate the warm sun and the gentle breeze."

Fourteen chimed in, "I don't think being a frog is such a great idea. I like my tail and love to swim about in the water. Can frogs swim?"

Number Twenty responded before I could reply. "Fourteen, don't you want to see what life is like on the other side of the waterline? Do you plan to compete as a swimmer in the tadpole Olympics? Open your mind."

Twenty-one tried to calm her siblings. "Look at old man up there, aren't you ashamed of yourselves? He is trying to help you understand the deeper meaning of life and all you can do is squabble."

The army froze at the observation. Clearly Twenty-one

was a respected leader, and not because of her assigned number. While Number Eleven had numerical positional authority, he lacked the wisdom to lead these tadpoles.

Number Twenty-one looked up at me, then back at her siblings. The army resumed their circular aquatic dance, but this time at a slower pace. She continued to speak.

"Sisters and brothers, I encourage you to also open your heart. I perceive that Vincent has seen his fair share of heartache and pain, but you need to understand how he writes through it all. He reveals recovery following loss."

At that moment, a chill ran up my spine. Twenty-one was the first of her kind to recognize my name. Did she know about my writings?"

Before I could speak, Twenty-one answered my thoughts.

"I know about every work you've written. I also know about all the books you've read. The one you're reading now connects the dots from your world to ours. I also know about the book you read last month. I know about ***Neverborn***. I get the connection between the novel and the novella that drives your thoughts."

"Do you really know my thoughts? When I read the novel, I tried to imagine your world. The opening chapter made me aware of your existence. That book also revealed a universe of never-born souls. They were denied an opportunity to experience life in human flesh. But they were able to speak to those who enjoyed that privilege.

"***Neverborn*** is a different kind of read. The never-born in that book examine the pain, loss and recovery that you attach to my life. My life has so many more stories of pain, loss and recovery. Jackson Badgenoone would need to write a whole series to capture all the events. But I must admit, I did connect with the way she introduces readers to the world of pain, loss and recovery. She opened the first chapter with an event that bore a striking parallel to a loss that impacted someone very close me. Here's what I read."

"The doctor glanced at the monitor. We made eye contact at the next moment, a moment that lasted for a lifetime.

"Mrs. Faith, Rachael, there is no heartbeat, I am so sorry."

Sorry didn't begin to describe what I felt when I heard those dreadful words.

This was the second time in as many years that I had heard that terrible message. When I lost a son last year, I went into a state of shock. For months following that stillbirth I sought comfort from other women who had experienced a similar silent moment.

I cried when I absorbed testimony on social media from so many other mothers who suffered a similar loss. I also pored over dozens of books that had sustained me in an earlier trial. Now another child, my child, wouldn't get to see the light of day. She wouldn't hear the sound of my voice. I wondered if the Lord had totally abandoned me. I put aside the books and I began to read the Bible from the very first book. Within a few hours, I came upon Exodus 23:25 (NIV).

> *'Worship the Lord your God and his blessing will be on your food and water. I will take away sickness from among you, and none will miscarry or be barren in your land. I will give you a full life span.'*

So, was it my fault? No, I knew that wasn't true, because

from the moment I accepted Jesus as my Savior, I have never stopped worshiping the Lord. There had to be another answer. For now I would have to rest in the Lord with the realization that my childbearing days may have drawn to a close. The following day my husband, Richard, and I left the hospital. We carried only a card of condolence and a mental image of our never-born daughter." ^{Page 1}

Number Nineteen left the circle and spoke to my heart.

"You humans are like that; you can mourn over the loss of what could have been. We tadpoles can only entertain the things that are. There is no room in this cranny life for imagination. Our days are consumed with the survival of those who swim in this shallow pool."

Number Twenty-one carried on the dialogue that assaulted my spirit.

"Nineteen, you need to speak for yourself. I imagine a world beyond this cranny. I often think about the brothers and sisters that never made it into our world."

"Yes, and you want to be a frog someday, don't you?"

"You miss the point, Nineteen. Options are limited. You can remain a tadpole and circle about until another flood washes you downstream. Or you can hope to live above the water-line, to embrace a more rewarding life. You need to move beyond existence."

Number Twelve joined the conversation. "Why do you squabble? Maybe we can learn a thing or two by listening to the thoughts of the old man. His species has the ability to write things down, to learn from previous generations, to instruct future generations. I for one am intrigued by this second book that considers the type of loss that humans face on their journey. Maybe we can learn from them. What say you, Vincent?"

"Yes, Number Twelve, you can learn from our trials and tribulations. Thank you for acknowledging my name. I get tired of being called the old man. I don't walk as fast as I once did, but my mind is young and my spirit is full of youthful joy.

"I was drawn to the second book because it revealed so many events that ran parallel to events in my life and the lives of immediate family and close friends. Jackson Badgenoone exposed the sorrow of several forms of pre-natal loss. She captured the horror of losing a young child in a car accident. She exposed the sorrow attendant to the loss of a spouse, a parent, a neighbor, and a friend."

"Which loss affected you the most?"

"Well, Nineteen, I suppose the loss of faith. At several points in the story, some of the characters just gave up. They lost their ability to see beyond the immediate pain. They blamed God for the tragedy that brought unwelcomed change into their lives.

Twenty-one rejoined the conversation. "I tried to explain that to Eleven and Fourteen. I encouraged them to look beyond their immediate circumstance, to believe that there is a better life waiting for them."

"Don't give up on that mission. Too bad you tadpoles can't form a book club. That's how Jackson brought a measure of closure to the loss experienced by some of the female characters in her book. In Chapter 28, Jackson set the stage for an expanded dialogue that created a deep-dive into the books they were reading."

[The principal character, Rachael, addresses her counterparts in that chapter.]

"I finally found the courage to speak. 'Ladies, we've endured pain and unspeakable sorrow. We've suffered miscarriage, stillbirth, abortion, rape, unwanted pregnancy, separation from our child, death of our child, loss of our spouse, burial of our parent, injustice meted out to our loved ones, and financial turmoil. This morning, Connie learned that her old neighborhood was affected by the earthquake.'

I thought, *spiritual conflict is a not an unexpected consequence of our travails.* We watched helplessly as our husbands tried to shield us from problems, and how they fell victim to the same hopelessness. We know other women who struggled with different burdens, those who never had a husband nor a child, no family or friends." Page 99

[In Chapter 31, Jackson encouraged the characters to expand the mission of their club. The chapter title provided a hint of what was to come. It was titled, A Broader Definition of Life. I continued to share Rachael's observation and the subsequent dialogue that unfolded in the story.]

"Jackson exposed the grief in the full range of tragedy that visited her family. She exposed different pathways to dealing with that grief."

Lydia spoke up. "Rachael, this book club really has morphed into something beyond the readings at hand. I am impressed by the way you ladies deal with adversity. You don't just talk the talk, you walk the walk. You reach out as a loving mom or daughter, a supportive sister or spouse, a literacy volunteer, a midwife, or a political activist.

Public and private sectors, we're all going to have to pitch in to bear our collective burdens. You have encouraged me in ways that you can't imagine and even have me framing my thoughts in Jacksonian nomenclature. I'm even starting to think like her." ^{Page 110}

[As the conversation continued to unfold, Rachael delivered a special message.]

"I know that you still struggle with the faith shared by the other women at this table. You argue with your inner voice about the injustice of a God who permits pain, suffering and death. My never-born children whisper to me. They tell me that, while they aren't affected by the toil, turmoil and drama of life, they long for the joy that life might have offered them." Page 112

"Number Twenty-one, we play on the same stage, just a different set."

Twenty-one assumed a position at the front of the circle. Eleven fell back to fill the vacated slot. Eleven still wasn't sure about how to handle all the new information. He was uncomfortable about the questions raised by his army buddies. A tear formed on my cheek when I realized that Number Eleven might never experience the full measure of life that was available to him.

In the next moment, a drop of rain touched my lips. Then another kissed my eye, yet another landed on my ear. The sky opened up, a new torrent replenished the creek.

Bibliography

The Hidden Treasure of Dutch Buffalo Creek, by Jackson Badgenoone—FriesenPress ISBN 978-1-4602-6735-6

The Hidden Treasure of Dutch Buffalo Creek - Heirloom Edition, by Jackson Badgenoone—FriesenPress ISBN 1-978-4602-7729-4

Neverborn, by Jackson Badgenoone—FriesenPress ISBN 978-1-5255-2297-0

About the Author

Vincent James Vezza is the first-born son of a career military officer. He grew up on Army bases around the world. Vincent holds a BA Degree in Political Science from Fairleigh Dickinson University and MS Degree in Education from Nazareth College. Following his studies, Vincent carved out a career in education, educational publishing, and educational technology. He sometimes writes under a pseudonym and encourages others to pick up the pen. You can learn more about Vincent at his website www.hiddentreasurenovels.com.

Made in the USA
Columbia, SC
24 March 2025